ISSUE 1

ELEMENTAL NINJA TECHS

OUT OF THE SHADOWS

DAVID KUMAH

ISSUE 1 | MIDDLE GRADE

Elemental Ninja Techs - Out of the Shadows (Issue 1)

ISBN: 978-1-916692-27-5

Cover/Layout Design
EQUIP PUBLISHING HOUSE

Published in the United Kingdom by
EQUIP PUBLISHING HOUSE

To Mum —You've always told me never to say "I can't," and because of you, I haven't. Your faith in me has been the fuel behind every challenge I've faced and every dream I've dared to chase. Your love, strength, and unwavering belief have shaped me into who I am. This book is as much yours as it is mine — born from the courage you taught me to carry.

To Mr. Lewis — More than a mentor, you have been a true father figure in my life. Your quiet strength, wisdom, and unwavering discipline have shaped not only how I think, but who I am becoming. Thank you for guiding me with integrity and care.

And to my incredible friends— Luke, Dainton, Elijah, Jayden, Elyse, Summer, Elvis, Austin, Zaydan, Jedidiah, Harry H, Charlie L, Charlie B, Ayaan, and Kian. Thank you for inspiring me, making me laugh, and standing by me through it all. I couldn't ask for better friends.

Contents

OUT OF THE SHADOWS P1

CHAPTER ONE

Out of the Shadows P1

It was another bright day, full of sun and sky, and yet it was still cold. Nothing out of the ordinary, just the usual long day of eighth grade, but this was the day a thirteen-year-old boy named Kyrin (Kai) Pax and his friends' lives would change forever.

An alarm suddenly started ringing loudly, waking Kai. The alarm clock startled him, but he knew he needed to hurry and get ready for school. He quickly grabbed his red Adidas hoodie, black shirt, and trousers out of the wardrobe in his apartment and put them on. He picked up his phone to check the time, realising he was almost late to meet up with his friends, Jet and Chloe Wilson. After a few minutes, he was ready to go, so he picked up his books and bag and left his apartment. On the way, he was texting on his phone, and then he passed by a fire hydrant. He put his phone back in his pocket and started to rub and blow on his hands.

Why can't today be warmer? He thought to himself. Suddenly, he started to feel weird. He felt warmer. Something was sparking inside him like he was on fire and burning, but it didn't hurt. Then he looked at his hands and realised they were glowing like an ember. He also felt his eyes were on fire. He could see, but he couldn't at the same time.

What's happening to me? Kai thought

A few seconds later, people were running in fear and screaming, "It's on fire. The fire hydrant is on fire!"

He turned around instantly and saw a blazing fire hovering over the fire hydrant. Without hesitating, he ran directly towards it, unnerved like someone else was in control. Then, he jumped, half a metre higher than he usually would, into the fire and absorbed the flaming energy into himself. When he landed on the ground, he was unscathed, and his clothes were not burned or scorched. Many of the people around him clapped and applauded him. In silence, he put his hood up and left. After that, whatever was happening to him instantly stopped and went away. Kai thought that the flaming sensation he was feeling inside him was somehow the cause of the fire. Luckily for him, he made it to school on time to see Jet and Chloe waiting for him in front of the school.

"Kai, you made it!" Jet said.

"What took you so long?" Chloe asked, annoyed.

"Hey Jet, hey Chloe. The strangest thing happened on the way here." Kai replied.

"Tell us at lunch. Class is about to start." Chloe said.

All of them went inside where the English class was about to start, but Kai was distracted. What happened? How did it happen? Things were getting weird for Kai, but they were about to get even more bizarre.

Jet was getting bored with English. He was going to make up some excuse to get out of it, but at that moment, his eyes transformed into a shamrock green colour. Kai and Chloe were the only ones to notice. While they looked at Jet in shock, the teacher's desk went green and slowly lifted off the floor. The teacher told everyone not to move, but one kid yelled, "What the heck is that!?"

The desk had transformed into an enraged animal. It started banging, crashing, and smashing everywhere, cracking windows and denting walls. All the students ducked underneath their desks, terrified; even the teacher cowered in the corner of the room. Everyone was afraid, but Kai was just confused. The desk was starting to glow greener and greener until it finally exploded, leaving ash marks on the floor. Kai looked over to see Jet's eyes turn back to their usual green hue. Just as things were calming back down, Chloe leaned over to reach for her water bottle and paused; She also started to feel a sense of unease, as if some change was about to happen, and her body did not know what to do. The colour of her eyes changed, not green like Jet's had, but the light blue colour of the ocean. A moment later, water leaked underneath the door. The teacher approached the door to open it, and as her hands reached out for the handle, a giant blast of water burst through the door, breaking it down and drenching every student that had been hiding underneath their desks. Chloe's eyes went back to normal, but the water had drenched everything and everyone in the room. Something weird was going on, and Kai was determined to find out what.

At lunch, Kai, Jet and Chloe were gathered at their lockers, determined to find out what was happening to them.

"So, you ran into a blazing fire, on a fire hydrant and lived to tell the tale?" Jet said, "Now I've heard everything."

"This is serious, Jet," Kai explained, looking around to see if anyone was listening.

"Why'd you call us here exactly?" Chloe asked.

"Because something weird is happening to us, and we need to find out what. Let us meet after school."

"Ok, let's do it." Jet agreed.

***

Meanwhile, three other classmates, Rocky Rhodes, Zach and Alex Bolteson, had detention for doing unexplained things at lunch. Whilst Rocky was playing basketball with others, he managed to evade the other players and made a shot, but missed. Furious, he stormed to a wall and punched it, but to his surprise, and that of the onlookers, the impact somehow created cracks in the wall until it crumbled down. Zach snuck into the security room to peer into the school network to find his and his brother's test results, where he somehow managed to absorb the electricity from the computers. Unfortunately for him, he was caught by the janitor just a few seconds after he absorbed the energy and reported him. Alex was walking down the hallway, but noticed that his hands were freezing like a raging blizzard, but it didn't hurt. He was trying to shake the feeling away and ended up accidentally making a frozen path on the floor, causing a teacher to slip and hurt their head. Each of them received an hour of detention after school. The boys were deeply puzzled what happened to each of them.

"You were looking for... your test results? How much of a nerd are you?" Rocky asked, raising his eyebrow.

"Hey, when you have a brain that is capable of hacking, let me know," Zach shrugged.

"You already know we're going to get another perfect score," Alex smirked.

"Anyways, I found something locked away in our father's private lab. It's a book about some heroes who had powers of Fire, Water, Energy, Ice, Earth and Electricity."

"Cool, wait, what does Earth do?" Rocky asked.

"Rock manipulation, dumb-dumb. Haven't you seen the movies?" Alex said. "And apparently, they have super strength as well."

"Well, we have three of those exact powers; we have to test them." Zach insisted.

"You're such a scientist," Rocky said, rolling his eyes.

"You think so?" Zach asked excitedly.

An hour later, the trio's detention was up. They went out on a mission to find a place to test out their newfound powers.

***

Meanwhile, Kai, Jet, and Chloe found an alley to test out their powers. Kai wanted to try first. He knew his powers were linked to fire, so he focused on heat. He felt that same flaming feeling he had before, and just like that, his hand was burning with a roaring flame. After witnessing Kai's results, Jet was eager to try. Kai thought his power was a type of green energy, so he told him to focus on energy. At that moment, Jet's hand started to glow green, and a big ball of energy formed and hovered over his hand. Next up was Chloe, who had influenced water in class, so she focused on the calm aspects of the ocean. Building moisture from the air around her, a whirlpool swirled around her hand. A moment later, they heard a noise around the corner. They left the alley to follow the source, running into a small crowd running from a blonde girl floating in a pink and blue suit.

"I am Crystal, I'm bored with New York's scenery, so I'll make it my Diamond palace," Crystal shouted and froze a man in crystals. Kai quickly put his hood up and ran over to free the man with his fire. Crystal saw this and was shocked.

"What! The element of fire! That's impossible!" She looked at Kai, angry and perplexed.

Five blocks over from the fight, Rocky, Zach, and Alex were talking about their powers when they heard Crystal's shouting.

"What was that?" asked Alex.

Rocky replied with a grin, "I don't know, but we're going to find out."

OUT OF THE SHADOWS P2

CHAPTER TWO

Out of the Shadows P2

Rocky, Zach and Alex ran over to see three people dodging a girl with crystal-powered attacks. The three people's powers matched the description of the ancient heroes in Zach's book.

"Jet, Chloe, let's try blasting her together," Kai said.

At that moment, Kai, Jet, and Chloe blasted a combination of fire, energy, and water at Crystal, but she fought back, freezing them in crystal cocoons.

"You three are a waste of my power," she laughed.

"We have to help them," Zach said.

"Listen up, I'll free them with my earth strength while you use your powers to buy me time. Got it?" asked Rocky.

They nodded and got into position. Zach and Alex both didn't know how their powers worked, but without hesitation, they directed precise shots of ice and electricity at Crystal. To protect those trapped in the cocoons, Rocky made an earth wall to shield them.

"Don't worry, I'll get you out," said Rocky, working to break Chloe's cocoon.

"Who are you?" Jet asked, his voice muffled by the crystal casing.

"Powered people like you," Rocky replied while breaking Kai's cocoon.

Finally, he broke the last cocoon. With all six of them, they had a chance to defeat Crystal. She must have known she had lost, because she quickly flew away. Without hesitation, the six chased after her. Crystal was fast, but the six were gaining on her. They were running on the streets, turning left and right, which led them to a small, out-of-use warehouse where her trail went cold. Considering the possibility that she had gone inside, they looked for a way in. Zach spotted a secret vent that was big enough for all of them to fit. One by one, they each went in, and what they found was amazing. Inside was a secret base with a giant high-tech computer, punching bags and weights, a large couch with a TV, a lift to a ground-floor level underneath, a training ring, and colour-coded lockers with their names on them. On a display cabinet sat six watches labelled "Tech Watches." Intrigued, Jet opened it, took a green one and put it on.

Zach, Alex and Chloe checked the computer. This warehouse appeared to be a top-secret base explicitly made for them.

Jet thought the watch was broken because it didn't do anything. He tapped it with two fingers and slapped it with the palm of his hand. With a flash, he was transformed. His Tech Watch had turned him into a green Ninja.

"Everyone needs to look at me right now," said Jet excitedly.

"Not now, big bro," Chloe said.

"Seriously, look!"

They turned around to see Jet in his Ninja Suit.

"Jet… what did you do?" Chloe asked, surprised.

"These Tech Watches. I think they transformed me, try them on. They have names on each of the cases."

Each of them grabbed their Tech Watches.

"What did you do exactly?" Kai asked.

"I tapped the watch once, then… Oh, I slapped it!" Jet explained.

After following Jet's instructions, they transformed, each wearing different coloured Ninja Suits. Kai's was red with a blue "Y" from the shoulders to the waist; Jet's was the same along with everyone else but his was green with a yellow "Y". Chloe's was light blue with a yellow "Y", Rocky's was black with an orange "Y" and Alex's was white with a blue "Y". Zach's however was different because he had a blue undersuit and blue, zip up vest with orange streaks at the top of it.

"This is legendary!" Rocky said, looking at the suit.

"Guys, check this out." Zach sat at the computer, his face illuminated by the screen. "I did some digging and found that we are some kind of superhero team called the Ninja Techs, and we have powers called the elements, but the main thing I found was this message." They leaned over his shoulder to read.

You are now the new, element-powered team: The Ninja Techs.

Your job is to defeat all threats to New York and protect all people from danger. These suits have many features that you can access on your Tech Bracer when transformed. I hope you unlock your full potential and achieve great success in the future.

Good luck, Ninja.

Suddenly, an alarm went off. Zach looked at the computer and saw that Crystal was back. She was crystallising people enough to make an army.

The Ninja Techs were ready to fight, but before they went, Jet stopped them, "Wait, wait, wait. If we are now butt-kicking heroes, we need names."

Kai called himself Inferno, Jet was now Psych, Chloe was now Wave, Rocky was now Quake, Zach chose the name Volt, and Alex was now Subzero. Now that they had their names, they were suited up and ready to protect New York.

3

CRYSTALLISED

CHAPTER THREE

Crystallised

Crystal had crystallised half of Midtown, but the Ninja Techs had arrived. Unfortunately, Crystal had expected and planned for this. She had made an army of Crystal Crushers. Volt and Wave were handling crowd control and getting innocent lives to safety. Quake was fighting against the military with Subzero. They stood back-to-back, blasting them with ice and earth. Inferno and Psych rapidly fired at Crystal, but she had made a shield to defend herself. Inferno saw bystanders in the path of an oncoming crystal. Instinct kicking in, he blasted the flying crystal with his fire, destroying the crystal and saving lives. Crystal's forces were growing. The Ninja Techs were getting beaten, but Inferno had an idea.

"Psych, you and I need to take out Crystal," said Inferno.

"How do we do that?" Psych asked.

"Give me a boost."

Using his powers, Psych made a platform. Inferno jumped onto the platform and boosted himself into the air. He clenched his flaming fist and was about to strike Crystal, but she sensed this and encased him on the wall of a building. When the team felt things couldn't get worse, Crystal absorbed the energy from some of her Crystal Crusher army and made a giant Crystal Titan. Psych then shot energy bolts at Crystal to distract her while the others came, but the rest of the team were held up with the Crystal Crushers. The odds of them winning were very low. The Ninja Techs were beginning to lose hope. But in that moment, three new Ninjas came in from the rooftops wearing different colours.

The first was wearing black with a golden Y-shaped pattern on the front and back, similar to the Ninja Techs. The second was wearing the same design, but his was red with a purple Y pattern. The third was wearing purple with a yellow Y. The Red and Purple Ninja used a telekinetic power to grab and hold the Titan's arms in place. Then, the Purple Ninja used animal-shifting powers to transform into a rhino and break the crystal wall shielding Crystal. The Golden Black Ninja transformed into a shadow-like mist to blind her. The Purple Ninja animal-shifted again into a T-Rex and chewed the Titan's head off. Finally defeated, Crystal was restrained by the Black and Gold Ninja. The Ninja Tech's first mission was a success. Crowds of people were clapping with joy, cheering on these mysterious heroes.

"We are here live on MNC with those being hailed, 'new heroes.' Please tell us who you are," the reporter said.

Inferno came to the front and said, "We're the Ninja Techs."

"And we're here to protect," Psych added.

They quickly jumped up on the roof to the other Ninja who had joined the fight.

"Thanks for the assist, but who are you?" asked Psych.

"I'm Ronin, the one in red and purple is my brother Neuro, and the one in purple and yellow is my sister Wildcard. We're the Resistance," Ronin explained. "We will take Crystal back to base and contain her. If you need us again, please feel free to call us. Oh, and we noticed you got here a little late, so take these teleport cards to get to places faster."

Inferno took them, but looked down at them, confused.

"You didn't know about them yet, did you?" Neuro asked.

"They are linked with the map on your computer and can teleport you anywhere in New York. You put them in your watches," Ronin explained.

"Thanks, Ronin. We need to get going," said Inferno.

The team then ran off, jumping from roof to roof.

"Until we meet again," Volt said, shouting in the distance.

Back at base, they transformed back. The mission was successful; they had gained new allies and gained more insight into their powers. The Ninja Techs were now eager to learn; they were ready for more.

DINE AND DANGER

CHAPTER FOUR

Dine and Danger

A few days later, Kai and Jet were hanging out at the base, training, when they got a call from Chloe.

"Hey guys. Wanna hang out with me and my friends?" she asked.

"Sure." They said in unison.

"Cool. Meet us at Toro's Feast."

She ended the call. Kai and Jet were confused as to why she asked them, of all people, to meet at Toro's Feast, but they didn't question it.

Kai and Jet got to Toro's Feast to find Chloe with two other girls.

"These are my friends Nikki Barlow and Zoey Hart. Girls, this is my brother, Jet and our friend Kai," Chloe told them.

Kai shook hands with Nikki, as did Jet with Zoey. They all went inside, got a table, and started ordering. Kai and Nikki decided to talk to each other and discovered they had a lot in common. Jet and Zoey tried to speak, but for some reason, it was awkward for both of them.

31

A moment later, Jet pulled Kai out to talk to him.

"Dude, I need to get out of this place. Could you please use your powers to make the smoke alarm go off?" Jet asked, "Then I can leave."

"Are you serious? Do you not like Zoey or something?" Kai asked.

"Do you not remember? We met her when we were kids, and she wasn't nice at all."

"I don't. Sorry, Jet, I would, but there are cameras everywhere."

They came back, and as they were about to sit back down, the food arrived. Suddenly, several armed thugs broke down the door and stormed in. Each thug was holding a loaded pistol, ready to fire. With the thugs distracting the crowd, Kai and Jet had a perfect opportunity to slip away and transform. They quickly ran into the bathrooms and came back out as Inferno and Psych. Everyone crouched under tables. Some were crying. A young couple held onto each other tightly with their eyes closed. Three of the thugs guarded a man Inferno and Psych took to be the leader of the ruffians, while he was threatening the waitress. Inferno and Psych knocked out two of the thugs.

"Sorry, Halloween's in ten months, kids. You're early," the second thug laughed, mocking Inferno and Psych.

"Wait, those are the Ninja Techs," warned the third thug.

"No really, what gave you that idea?" said Inferno.

Ticked off, the thug ran at Inferno, raising his gun as he stormed toward him. Inferno kicked the gun out of his hands before he could fire. Psych blasted the rest into a wall, but these guys had called for backup. They all shot at the two of them. Psych quickly made a shield with his powers. Without hesitation, Inferno leapt overhead and melted all the guns with a blast of fire.

"Freaks! Let's get out of here!" shouted the leader.

"Too easy!" Psych laughed.

"Now use the smoke bomb," Inferno whispered.

Psych selected the smoke bomb on his Tech Bracer, transported it, and threw it on the ground. While transforming back, Nikki saw a flash of their identities but didn't say anything.

They went back to the table to make sure everyone was okay. On their way out of Toro's Feast, Kai stopped Nikki.

"Nikki, I think you and I have a lot in common. Do you want to hang out sometime, just you and me?" he nervously ran his hands through his hair.

Nikki smiled, "Sure, meet me at the top of the building here."

***

Kai had decided to use his powers to hurry to the rooftop where he planned to meet Nikki. He jumped from roof to roof until he was close to the building. When he got there, he silently landed next to the door on the roof, transformed back, then opened and closed the door to make it sound like he came out of there.

"Hey Nikki," Kai smiled.

"Hi Kai," she replied.

"Why'd you pick here?"

"I wanted no one to find us."

Kai nervously walked up to her.

"So, I wanted to tell you that I…"

"That you are Inferno."

"What?"

"I saw you and Jet transform. Don't worry, I'm not going to tell anyone."

"I was going to say that I like you and I wanted to ask if you would want to go out with me?"

Nikki looked surprised but smiled. "I don't know. Don't get me wrong, I do like you, it's just that we just met, and I just found out you are a superhero, and it's dangerous to date a superhero. I promise I'll think about it."

Kai's watch beeped. It was an emergency alert.

"I've got to go. Bye, Nikki." Nikki waved, and Kai, in a rush, quickly teleported to base.

NEW ENEMIES, NEW SOLUTIONS

CHAPTER FIVE

New Enemies, New Solutions

There was an emergency call happening. The Resistance's base was being attacked, so the Ninja Techs logged in the coordinates and teleported to their base.

The Resistance's base had everything the Ninja Techs had, but with more tech and a different colour scheme. They didn't have time to look around because some weird shadow-energised creatures were lurking.

"What are they?" Quake asked.

"Let's call them…. Shifters!" Psych replied.

"Good name, but now's not the time," Inferno said.

A mysterious monster wearing a cloak and teal-coloured robot helmet with pointy ears led the Shifters.

"Well, hello, Ninja." The monster's voice was robotic, but it maintained a human quality about it.

"Who are you?" Inferno asked, keeping his guard up.

"Your native tongue cannot pronounce my name, so you may call me Kanzorum."

"Hello, Kanzo, welcome to Earth. Hope you don't enjoy your visit." Psych said. He blasted him with an energy bolt.

The Ninja Techs and the Resistance worked together, using their powers to battle these invaders. They managed to push the fight outside of the base.

With space and less of a risk of destroying the base, Volt hit the Shifters with an immense amount of electricity, disrupting their energy and causing them to explode. Things were looking good. Inferno was heating things up against all the Shifters. Kanzorum almost looked worried as he watched Inferno use his powers.

"The fiery one is the Universal Master's successor. But that's impossible. Send in Raven," Kanzorum shouted.

"Universal Master?" Quake said while punching a Shifter.

Inferno was confused, but there was no time to process this information, because a girl in a dark purple Ninja suit and a cloak slashed a giant scythe at him. Inferno hit her back with intense fire blasts, but the girl knew what she was doing. With her scythe, she sliced Inferno's blast in half, causing one half to hit a car and explode. The girl slowly marched into Inferno, raising her scythe in the air, preparing to put an end to him permanently. Eye to eye with this mysterious girl, Inferno had a feeling she was familiar to him.

Just then, Psych shot her with an energy blast, knocking her back deeply into a building. Danger temporarily averted, he tried hard to think back to when he was younger, about seven years old. His memories from that time were hazy, but her powers were the same as the ones his little six-year-old sister had when he trained with his dad. Inferno questioned his memories and soon began to wonder why he had not known about his powers sooner. He had to figure that out later because they were losing. He saw the situation around him. Psych and Wave were on the floor and about to be struck by Kanzorum. Shifters overran Volt and Quake. Inferno started to feel overcome with the fear of losing his team, but then he felt something overcome him. His eyes changed to the colour of the universe itself. It felt as if fear and anger were in control. Instead of fire, a dazzling spectrum of gold, blue, red, purple, and pink energy erupted in a powerful blast. Single-handedly, he took out every one of the Shifters with a single blast. Kanzorum and Raven escaped just before the explosion hit, but next time, they would be ready, and so would the Ninja Techs.

After that, Inferno went back to normal, but he was weak. Although his body told him he needed rest, Inferno had too many questions that needed answers. He teleported back to base, leaving the rest of the team behind. Back at base, Kai started looking up all the element types on the main computer. He found more and more about the elements that he couldn't imagine, but that wasn't the information he needed right now. He stopped when he saw a section on the

Universal Element. The Universal Element was one of a kind because it was exclusive to his family. The ability to wield it always goes to the firstborn, which was Kai in his family. The Universal Element was every single powerful element that existed combined into one, making it the most potent element in the universe. To use it on command, Kai would need to learn the six most powerful elements in order: Ice, water, earth, electricity, energy and fire. Kai would need his friends to teach him the basics. When the rest finally came back to base, Kai immediately told them everything he had learnt, then asked Alex if he could teach him how to master ice, but Alex said he was not a master yet. Alex explained, "While you and Jet were at Toro's Feast, yeah Chloe told us, Zach and I researched that each generation of the Ninja Tech Teams are connected because a part of your universal energy is inside us and when the first elemental in the cycle, masters the basic knowledge of their power the connection is active making it easier to train you."

Alex had just started, along with everyone else, which meant they were all still novices. At that moment, Kai remembered the scroll he had seen when they first found the base. He thought it could perhaps provide them with more knowledge and help them become masters. The others followed Kai as he ran to a cabinet labelled "Art of the Jutsu", where they found the Tech Scroll. Kai unravelled it. At first, it appeared blank. Then, slowly, crystal blue writing materialised.

Kai read it aloud,

"You have proven with your skill and determination that you are ready for the next level of your training. In this Tech Scroll, you will learn all Jutsus corresponding to the skill level recorded in your Tech Bracer. Keep the scroll so you may access more Jutsus in time. At your level, these are the following you will learn: Dragon Jutsus, the Jutsu of summoning your dragon and Elemental Burst Jutsu, the hardest of all. It is a Jutsu only you six can use. It will supercharge your element with the power of universal energy."

"Guys, we have to try this out!" Jet said excitedly.

Chloe and Rocky decided to do Dragon Jutsu. They got into position and said the words, "Dragon Jutsu!"

Light blue and black colours swirled around before two dragons formed in front of them. One with midnight black scales and an orange saddle, the second with light ocean blue scales and a yellow saddle.

"Awesome! Actual dragons!" Chloe said, hugging the dragon, "I'm going to name you Tsunami!"

"And I'm going to name you Earth Walker," Rocky said, petting Earth Walker.

"Kai, you should try the last one," Zach said.

Kai was nervous. He thought that if Element Burst Jutsu was the hardest element to master, it would be very unpredictable and could injure everyone in the room.

"Yeah. If anyone can do it, you can," Jet smiled.

"Ok. Let's do it," Kai said.

Kai got into position, but when he said, "Fire Burst Jutsu!" Nothing happened.

Zach checked the scroll to see what had happened, and more words materialised on the scroll. It read,

"Only in a time of extreme measures will you be able to invoke the elemental burst. Once achieved, you will gain the title of an Elemental Master."

Kai was disappointed but relieved that he couldn't use it.

Moments later, scanners detected someone teleporting into the base.

6

MEMORIES AND NIGHTMARES

CHAPTER SIX

Memories and Nightmares

Preparing to fight, the Ninja Techs had their powers charged up and ready to blast. To their surprise, the creature that appeared happened to be a brown dog. The Ninja Techs were very confused. Jet laughed, but then the dog shapeshifted into a human – a teen about their age. Jet stopped laughing, the jovial expression on his face replaced with a dropped jaw. He had tanned skin and dark brown hair, slicked back, wearing a grey, red, and yellow trench coat.

"Hey Ninja Techs, name's Ryku, Ryku Mesagon. I'm a friend of yours," he said. "You would know me, Kai."

Kai thought something was familiar about Ryku, just like when he fought with that Raven girl. At that moment, he had a flashback to a memory of a younger version of him, Jet and a kid who looked just like him playing together. He then realised that this was his childhood friend.

"Oh…My…God! Ryku! Is that you?" Kai said happily.

"Wait, Ryku?!" Jet said excitedly.

"Kyrin Pax, good to see you, old friend. You too, Jet," Ryku said.

"Ryku, it's been a while," Jet laughed.

Kai and Jet introduced the others to Ryku, but they were more focused on where and why he came.

"I'm an Elemental, technically. I live on the moon of the planet from which the original elements came. My home is called Yavara. I can shapeshift into anyone and anything in the universe. I came to warn you—a monster from Titan's Core invaded my home, Voragon. He is a horned demon-like warrior— the son of the most feared monster in the galaxy, Kilojav. He has wiped out everything on my planet with the help of Kanzorum and Voragon's daughter, Raven, the Elemental of Dark Magic. Now I'm the only one left."

The Ninja Techs had previously faced Kanzorum and Raven in their last battle. Since then, Zach had developed scanners to detect abnormal criminal activity or danger, just in case the duo returned. And right on cue, the scanners activated. Kanzorum and Raven had arrived in downtown Greenwich. The Ninja Techs transformed.

Raven had brought an army of Shifters to attack. When they got there, Inferno felt that feeling again when he saw Raven. The sensation paralysed him. He couldn't focus on the fight. To him, finding out how

Raven fit into his past was crucial to defeating her. A Shifter was about to blast Inferno with a shadow bolt, but Inferno was still too distracted to defend himself.

Psych noticed that Inferno was unguarded and quickly made a sphere around him. Quake stomped his foot onto the ground, and it arose, creating a spike wall that impaled the Shifters in front of it. Wave, however, was using her element to make tentacle-like arms to whip the Shifters.

Inferno suddenly recognised her—the element, the appearance, the fighting style. This was no stranger. It was his little sister, Ravena!

Quake was blasting giant rocks at each Shifter he encountered. Subzero and Wave teamed up and blasted waves with some water-ice combos. Volt targeted each of the Shifters and blasted electricity at every Shifter he marked. Psych's shield around Inferno was starting to break. As soon as it did, he created a new one with himself inside.

"What's going on?" Psych nudged Inferno on the shoulder and looked at him with concern.

"Raven," Inferno's gaze followed her moves, "She is my sister."

Inferno thought that if Raven didn't recognise him the way he did for her, then he could show her that memory. With that idea in mind, Inferno devised a plan. He first shared it with Psych, then contacted Neuro through the communicator on his Tech Bracer to bring him in as well.

"Alright, team, hold her down and trap her!" Inferno shouted.

Quake encased her arms and legs in stone, then Psych added an energy layer for a strong defence.

"Look, I know you don't trust us, but please, sis, remember who you were, remember who you are," Inferno said.

"You're right, I don't trust you and I will kill you," she threatened and then she freed herself from the stone. They quickly added more stone and energy layers with an ice layer on top while Inferno called for backup. Then Ronin's brother, Neuro, teleported to their location. Inferno focused on the memories he had with himself and Raven, then Neuro transferred those memories from him to Raven. Raven felt weak and uneasy with the new memories in her head. She was startled by the realisation that she was fighting on the wrong side.

"I...I remember, Kai! Is it you?" Raven asked.

"Yes, Ravena, it's me," Inferno smiled.

Kanzorum, enraged that they converted his best fighter to their side, blasted them with dark energy.

"Psych, shield up!" Inferno shouted.

Psych did as he said and created a shield just before the blast hit. Subzero transported a smoke bomb and threw it to the ground. With Kanzorum blinded, the Ninja Techs quickly escaped with Raven.

Kanzorum snarled as he stumbled out of the smoke.

He radioed back to the homeland, "They took Raven. And we have another problem. The Universal Master has returned."

A TRICK AND TROUBLE

CHAPTER SEVEN

A Trick and Trouble

Kai was so happy to have his little sister back that he decided she could stay in the base or his apartment for now. Raven told them that they should start preparing because Kanzorum would have a plan to destroy them. She would never be allowed to be a part of it, but she knew it would be something bad. Jet and Rocky, feeling the need to prepare, attempted to train to unlock new power skills. Zach and Ryku went to the lab to prepare new tech weapons, and Alex and Chloe worked to train their dragons.

Kai, however, went out to relax. He left the base in a little bit of a hurry and headed down to a nearby shop to buy some food. A shrill scream stopped him in his tracks. He ran around the corner to find a brown-haired girl cowering away from a Shifter. Kai ran to her rescue, side-kicking the Shifter in the face. On impact, the Shifter disappeared into a cloud of purple dust.

"That thing was going to kill me! Thank you." She smiled and shook his hand, "I'm Paige. And you are?" she asked.

"I'm Kyrin, Kyrin Pax, but you can call me Kai," He replied.

At that moment, more Shifters started to appear further down the street.

"I've got to go," Kai said apologetically before running toward the Shifters.

Kai sent an emergency alert to the base as he transformed. As Inferno stood, ready to fight, the rest of the team showed up fully suited. At the same time, Kanzorum made his appearance. He was armoured in a heavily equipped Tech Suit. Volt activated his visor and began scanning the suit. He sent the scan data back to the base computer.

"Shifters, attack!" Kanzorum yelled.

In a flash, electricity and fire bolts were shot in a flurry of attacks at dozens of Shifters. Psych flipped over three of the Shifters and created a cricket ball with his powers.

"The amazing Psych about to bowl out three Shifters." Psych adopted an announcer tone. He stepped back and threw the ball, hitting all three of the Shifters, "And the incredible cricket champion, Psych, strikes out the losers."

Wave used her tentacle-arm move to whip the Shifters. Then she grabbed hold of a dozen Shifters and spun them round and round like a turbine. When she let them go, they flew into the sky. Subzero encased them in ice as they came back down.

Kanzorum looked on, unimpressed. "I've seen better form from lesser beings," he scoffed.

"Believe me, Kanzo, you're about to see the main event." Inferno grinned, charging up the flame energy in his hands.

Following Inferno's lead, the Ninja Techs unleashed a powerful beam of all their elemental forces at the suit. Kanzorum's clothes were scorched, his strength drained, and he stood defenceless—yet he didn't act like it. He was laughing.

"Thank you, Ninja. I have what I need," he smirked.

Before the Ninja Techs could process what he meant, he had disappeared.

"What did he mean by 'I have what I need?'" Psych looked to Inferno for answers.

"I don't know," Inferno looked at the space where Kanzorum had stood, "but I think we need to figure it out fast."

DOOMSDAY DILEMMA

CHAPTER EIGHT

Doomsday Dilemma

When the Ninja Techs got back to base, Ryku and Raven were already worried.

"What happened?" Jet asked.

"Kanzorum's new armour?" Ryku sighed.

"Yeah, what about it?" Kai asked.

"Well, Volt had scanned it with his visor and sent us the data. When you hit him with your elemental energy, the armour recorded and absorbed its energy, and now he's going to use the data on the armour, upload it to a doomsday device that will force the elemental energy to unearth from Earth's core, and break the planet from the inside!"

"How do you know?" Kai asked.

"I linked up with Kanzorum's system when I had the data from the armour and found the design for the plans," Ryku explained.

Zach went up to the computer, pulled up a map of New York, and pinpointed Kanzorum's location. It showed that Kanzo and the device were at the top of Pearl Tower.

"Let's kick Kanzo's butt," Jet said with a smirk.

The Ninja Techs made it to Pearl Tower as Kanzo was prepping the Doomsday Device. Kanzo had a massive army of Shifters ready. Psych dodged blasts left and right and returned the fire with some energy bolts. Inferno and Quake were distracting Kanzo so he wouldn't catch Volt hacking the Doomsday Device. After analysing the data, Volt concluded that the device had been infused with an unrecognised, corrupted, and volatile energy. If Volt shut it down, the device would activate that energy, and it could explode the entire city. Volt figured the only way to stop it was to destroy it with the same energy it recorded in the first place. The elemental energy would cancel out its power and contain the blast. Psych could contain the explosion at the top of Pearl Tower? It was a risky move, but the options were limited.

"Guys," Volt's voice remained calm.

"Kinda busy here!" Psych shouted, fending off five Shifters.

"The only way to stop it is to destroy it with the same blast we hit Kanzo with," Volt explained.

"Right," Quake said.

"Psych, you have to contain the blast at all costs," Volt told Psych. "Can you handle it?"

"I'll try," Psych replied. He rubbed his hands together.

They all made their way to the Device. Psych made an energy sphere around them and the device. Kanzo and the Shifters blasted the shield with everything they had, but Psych's skill was improving, and the sphere held. The Ninja Techs were ready. They focused all their energy into their element and blasted a combined energy burst, which demolished and exploded the device. The roof caved in, and rubble littered the area.

Dust and smoke filled the air, but Kanzo and the Shifters saw the big hole where the Ninja Techs were standing. Kanzo thought they were dead. He had finally defeated the Ninja Techs—but in a flash, Quake rebuilt the rooftop with his earth powers, and they teleported themselves to the repaired roof. The first thing they saw was little, fuchsia coloured energy particles in the air.

Kanzo laughed.

"Why are you laughing? We destroyed the device?" Volt asked.

"Yeah, what's so funny?" Inferno asked. Kanzo's reaction reminded him of their previous mistake. He had reacted the same way when they had blasted that suit. They must have made a mistake once again.

"Thank you, Ninjas, for volunteering. You did all the work for us." He laughed, then disappeared.

The Ninja Techs were left confused, but if Kanzo were telling the truth, they would find out what he was talking about soon enough.

CHAPTER NINE

Welcome to Element City P1

A week had passed since the Doomsday Device was destroyed. School was out for the day, and not a single villain or Shifter was anywhere in sight.

Kai and Paige sat together at Antonio's Diner.

It started well, and they were having fun together.

People began falling to the ground. Kai stood up and turned around to see people groaning on the floor, looking like they were about to be sick. The wave of illness shifted, rising from the ground, as elemental power emanated from the crowd. Soon after, they were using elemental powers. Water, energy, earth, ice, electricity and fire - one of each of the Ninja Tech's powers shot from the people's fists.

Paige was freaked out, but not as much as Kai. Kai learned that only the Elemental Masters' descendants can use the power of the elements. Kai assumed that this was what Kanzorum meant when they destroyed the machine, and somehow their powers spread throughout the whole city. The particles in the air changed everyone in the city into elemental people.

"Paige, I'm sorry I have to go," he said.

"Wait, before you go, can I get your number?" Paige asked, "You know… so we can talk again?"

"Sure," he replied, then quickly gave it to her and left.

Kai ran outside and quickly ducked into an alleyway before teleporting to base.

"Guys, something's gone wrong!" Kai exclaimed.

"We know. Element-powered people are popping up everywhere," Zach said.

"They have our powers. Is that a good thing?" Alex asked.

"I wouldn't think so," Ryku replied, "People could seriously hurt themselves. Kai, what do you think?"

"We don't have a way to stop it, so we should monitor it and see what happens."

Chloe was on a call with Nikki and Zoey. They said they woke up with powers, but theirs were different to the ones everyone else had. Nikki had a magic type of ability, and Zoey could move through walls like it was an open door. Ryku figured that they were descendants of elementals, but their powers were dormant, and the particles from the device awakened them.

"This may go wrong, so everyone should look out for anything suspicious," Kai said.

Jet and Chloe went back to the park to chill out. Ryku, Zach, and Alex were reviewing the designs for the Doomsday Device. Rocky went to the courts to play some basketball, and Kai called Paige, telling her to meet him back at Antonio's Diner. When he got back, he saw that the people were using their powers like they'd had them all their lives. The cooks in the kitchen heated and cooked everything they made over their fire. Others were using the water element to put the drinks in their mouths. Others used the earth to move things or themselves around.

What the people didn't realise was that the powers they were using had the capability of levelling the city. The thought filled Kai with trepidation, but, for the moment, he decided to relax and enjoy his time with Paige. A few hours later, Kai and Paige were heading home for the day when they came across a thug robbing a lady of her purse. Kai was about to do something when the cops came hovering in with their firepower. The thug was quickly apprehended. Kai was beginning to think that maybe having powers by everyone was a good thing.

"Thanks for walking with me back home, Kai," Paige smiled.

"Anytime, Paige," Kai smiled back.

"And I wanted to say again, thanks for saving me."

"It was nothing."

"You're such a great guy."

Paige wrapped her arms around his neck, hugging him tight like she didn't want him to leave. After the long embrace, she waved goodbye and ran inside. Kai walked back to base with a grin on his face.

When he got there, the team's faces were blank.
They didn't know how to feel now that the city no
longer needed them.

"Anything strange happening?" Kai asked.

"The people I was playing basketball with invented
a new game of basketball with the Earth element,"
Rocky said. "So, you tell me."

"Let's go home, it's been a long day."

The next day, Inferno was running on the roofs
of buildings, trying to find things to do. He sat on
the ledge of a building when he heard an explosion
a few blocks away. He leapt over buildings, trying to
find out where the explosion was coming from. He
jumped down and landed on a lamp post when he saw
someone walking to a flipped-over armoured truck.
He activated his visor to get a better look at the guy.
He appeared to have two bionic arms and an electrical
reactor in his chest. Inferno jumped down, landing on
the flipped truck.

"Hey, Metal Man, do you have a name, or do I call
you Trash Can?" Inferno said.

"Hello Inferno, my name's Daniel Jones, but you
can call me Bionic." He said, charging up for a fight.
He shot a blast from his right arm, but Inferno jumped
up and dodged it before the shockwave hit. Inferno
recognised this kind of blast. This was Volt's electricity.
It enabled Bionic's arms to wield elemental and
technologically powered weapons. Inferno threw balls
of fire to hit the power source, but like Volt, Bionic's

power and the reactor had a shielding effect. Bionic then launched his arms at Inferno like tentacles, trying to hit him. Inferno was dodging the attacks, but he needed help. He was about to call the rest of the team when Bionic blasted electricity into Inferno's Tech Bracer. The blast blocked all his communication systems. Luckily, at that moment, a guy with a brown fauxhawk and dressed in a black suit came in to help, blasting fire at Bionic.

"Pleasure to meet you, Inferno," The guy smiled.

Inferno didn't say anything but stared at him in shock. Bionic got back up and smacked the guy into the truck. As he eased out of the body-shaped dent he made in the truck, he commanded, "On three, target the core and blast him with everything you've got!"

"Remember, the Ninja Techs fight to defeat, not to kill," Inferno said while dodging Bionic's tentacle-like arms.

"If he has electrical energy, then I could use some new tech Volt cooked up and get a blast of his electricity. I could latch on to and drain the rest from the reactor."

Bionic's reactor glowed a lapis blue. His arms were sparking with electricity. Unfazed, Inferno transported the Electric Latch and flipped it into position.

"You'll be shocked at what I will do next," Bionic said.

He blasted his energy directly at Inferno, but nothing happened. The Latch activated, and the shockwave was trapped. Bionic could not move, nor could he use his powers; the reactor's glow began to fade as the Latch drained the power. With his power completely drained, Bionic collapsed to the floor. He swung his fist at Inferno, trying to punch him, but he was too weak. After a few weak swings at the air, Bionic collapsed into unconsciousness.

"Oh, your batteries are dead. You should get new ones," Inferno smirked at his joke.

He went to shake the hand of the guy who helped him.

"My name is Lance Hughes, a powered person hired to use my new power for the good of the U.S. I'm the first of many soon to come super soldiers," Lance said.

"Wait, super soldiers?" Inferno asked.

"That's correct. The society I work for hired a scientist who experimented with powers like mine. He is working to create a serum to give to army soldiers that will enhance them with elemental abilities."

"You can't! These powers are dangerous and should be used with caution!"

"It's not up to you, kid. This is for the good of the world."

"As the original user of these powers, I know what they can do and how much damage they can cause."

Lance was annoyed at Inferno, but didn't bother to argue with him. He used his firepower to blast himself away from the area.

Inferno rebooted his systems, and his communications were back. A few seconds later, he got a call from Paige.

"Hey Kai, are you busy?" Paige asked over the phone.

"No, I just finished what I'm doing," Inferno said.

"Are you okay? You sound annoyed."

"It's nothing."

"If you say so, Kai. Meet me at Toro's Feast, 8 o'clock."

"Have to tell the team about the super soldiers," Inferno said to himself. He activated his Tech Bracer to transport a grapple glove, and then he swung away.

***

Kai made it to Toro's Feast on time, where he saw Paige already at a table waiting for him. Kai sat down at the table.

"So, why'd you call me here?" Kai asked.

"If you're busy with something, we can talk another time," Paige's grin turned down.

"No, that's ok. Sorry, just had something else on my mind before I got here." He smiled to assure her he was happy to be there.

"I just wanted to talk and get to know you better." Paige said, smiling, "What do you like doing?"

"I like hanging out with my friends, Jet and Chloe. I also love making beats."

"Oh, you make music?"

"I do it in my spare time. How about you, what do you like to do?"

Paige thought for a moment.

"Well, I love music, but I mostly love to dance. Maybe I can dance to your music," she laughed. "Now the most important question right now: are you ready to eat?" Paige grinned.

"Yes!" Kai laughed.

The chef came to the table performing a water and fire show with their elemental powers. After the show, the waiter came with spicy chicken, salad and chips, which was today's special, along with pain au chocolate and croissants for dessert. After eating for ten to fifteen minutes, it was getting dark and very late, so Kai walked with Paige back home. On the way home, Paige asked Kai more questions and started to feel more comfortable around him.

***

"I'm telling you I've seen them live," Kai laughed. They walked side by side toward Paige's home.

"No, you haven't!" Paige smiled.

"My dad took me because my sister, Ravena, wanted to see them live."

"Ok, Kai, I believe you." She stopped in front of her apartment building. "Well, this is my stop. See you later?"

"Of course, can't wait."

Paige hugged him and waved goodbye before heading into the building. On his way back to the apartment, he spotted a man in a grey hoodie standing motionless in an alley, frozen in place.

"Um, excuse me, are you ok?" Kai asked, but the hair on his neck stood up. Something was wrong.

WELCOME TO ELEMENT CITY P2

10

Welcome to Element City P2

When Kai raised his hand to tap him on the shoulder, the man instantly pulsed with electricity running through his veins. His eyes became as white as pearls. His power corrupted him, and he became something else entirely. His entire body crackled with glowing cobalt-blue electricity. Kai instinctively leapt back in fear.

Meanwhile, Jet and Chloe, who were walking around the park, saw the same thing happening to the people around them. Some with fire powers turned into crimson and orange flaming humanoids, while the people with earth had dirt and stone-textured skin with vines wrapping around them to complete the look. An emergency meeting at the base was called immediately. Ryku, Subzero, and Volt looked at the Doomsday Device designs and concluded that the unrecognised energy must be Kanzo's corrupted powers. His energy corrupted the people, and their powers combined to create an elemental monstrosity.

While the team deliberated on how to handle this new dilemma, Kai got a phone call. It was Paige.

"Kai, you have to come quickly. These people turned into glowing things and are trying to break into my apartment!" she screamed before the call ended.

"Guys, I need to go," Kai said, leaping to his feet.

"Be careful, Kai," Jet said.

He nodded, then ran through the holographic exit.

"Ok, listen up. Kai's gone. We must control the situation," Jet told the team, "Ideas?"

"Zach and I can make an anti-doomsday device, but without the original plans, we can't find out how to reverse it." Ryku explained, "We could send three of you to go get them. I need to find out where they're being held.

"Then we all agree that Zach, Kai and I, if he gets back here, will get the plans, while Chloe, Alex, and Rocky will get the corrupted people to one large place?" Jet asked.

The Ninja Techs nodded. Kai made it to Paige's apartment, but it was overrun. Kai kicked the door open but realised that was a mistake when he saw how many people were corrupted. The moment he came in, the corrupted were walking to him like zombies. They blasted shots of their elements at him, but Kai was moving like the wind as he swiftly dodged them and returned fire. The corrupted had poor aim and slow reaction. Kai swiftly moved past them, making his way up to Paige's room. Kai knocked on the door, but no response. He knocked again.

"Go away, monsters!" Paige shouted.

The corrupted were making their way up the stairs. Kai shot fire bolts at them, but there were too many, and the corrupted with fire power were absorbing his blows.

"Paige, open up! I can't hold them off!" Kai said, struggling to keep them all back.

Paige opened the door, and she closed it, but Kai shot a fire bolt, knocking the corrupted down the steps just before she did.

"You have powers, too," Paige said. "Why aren't you like them?"

"Why aren't you also like them? It corrupted everyone from Harlem to the Financial District?" Kai asked.

"I was in Brooklyn at the time it happened. But you still haven't answered my question, Kai."

Before Kai could answer, he got a hologram message from Jet on his Tech Watch.

"You were going to find out sooner or later." Kai sighed and played the message.

"Kai, we have a plan. Get to base. We'll fill you in when you get there," Jet told him.

Kai quickly activated his Tech Watch and transformed.

"Oh my god, you're... you're one of the Ninja Techs... from the news!" Paige stared at him, shocked.

"I'm Inferno, and my friends need me, so we've got to get out of here and get to base."

"Ok Ka… I mean Inferno, let's go!"

Inferno led Paige to the window and opened it; they both jumped out of it, then Inferno quickly said, "Dragon Jutsu!"

His dragon, Heatblast, appeared in a flash. He helped Paige mount the dragon before jumping on behind her. As Heatblast landed, the Techs glared at the unexpected guest in their secret domain.

"Kai, you brought your girlfriend," Jet sighed.

"I'm not his girlfriend, I'm his friend, and you must be Jet. Kai told me about you."

Jet walked over to Kai and wrapped his arm around his shoulders.

"I thought no one was supposed to know our identities, superhero 101," Jet whispered.

"I couldn't just leave her. I was in a rush to get here," Kai whispered back.

"Ok, if you can trust her, then I'll trust her."

"Anyway, we found some information," Zach interrupted.

"We looked over the Doomsday Device designs again. It turns out the design we had was a fake. The Doomsday Device was a dispersion unit filled with Elemental DNA from ours and Kanzo's energy."

"In English, please," Jet sighed.

"It was designed to corrupt people. There should be a drive with enough data to recreate the container in the lab. We need to get the drive to rebuild the container. Ryku and I can easily create reversed DNA like this is a chemistry lesson."

"You'll find it on Kanzo's ship," Ryku added.

Jet, Kai, and Zach activated their Tech Watches and transformed. After that, they went to the computer to scan for Kanzo's Airship. They quickly found it, camouflaged above Pearl Tower. They were ready, but before they left, Ryku downloaded an update to their suits. It was for an x-ray they could access with their visors to look for cloaked objects, see through walls and could even download the images back to the base. Once the update finished downloading, they were ready to retrieve the file and make their exit. The rest decided that the best place to gather the corrupted was Central Park. Quake, Subzero, and Wave ran out of the base to search for the corrupted. Inferno, Psych, and Volt made it to Pearl Tower and activated their visors to see the ship. Psych blasted himself and Inferno boosted up to the ship, while Volt used the grapple glove to get up to it. They walked around the corridors, cautiously and slowly, to avoid detection. Shifters were marching everywhere, so Inferno figured they should split up and meet back at the entrance to the ship.

"If anyone finds the drive, report on comms," he whispered.

Volt went up in the vents. He crawled around for a while, feeling like he was going in circles, just then he overheard Kanzo talking with someone.

"My Lord, there have been some issues with the plan," Kanzo stammered.

"If you cannot get rid of some children, then I will rid them and you myself," The other said.

"But my Lord, the Universal Master has a successor."

"That's... impossible."

"They must be talking about Kai," Volt whispered to himself. He crawled forward to reach the source of the voices. As he planted his knee, the metal underneath him groaned.

"What was that?" the other bellowed angrily. Kanzo's superior walked toward the air vent, catching a glimpse of Volt's blue suit before Volt could back away. "Find him."

Inferno and Psych heard an alarm go off, and they saw Shifters coming down the hall. Volt quickly called Inferno and Psych on the communication line.

"So, don't get mad, I think they may have seen me... but I got some intel," Volt said.

"Like?" Inferno asked, annoyed that he got caught.

"That Kanzo was talking with who I assume is his leader, and that they are afraid of you because you're the successor to the Universal Master."

"Everywhere we go, that title keeps coming up," Inferno sighed.

While they were talking, Psych found the drive in the computer room. "Ok, I've got it, now let's bolt."

Meanwhile, Quake, Wave, and Subzero managed to get all the corrupted people in one place. Some were trying to escape. The quake shook the ground. It arose, making a wall around half of Central Park while Subzero and Wave combined their powers to finish the wall, creating a barrier that the corrupted could not escape. Once they finished, they went back to base and waited for Inferno, Psych, and Volt to come back with the drive.

Inferno and the rest made it out of the airship with the drive. Volt shot a zipline down to the ground. Kanzo was right behind them. He spoke in another language. It reminded Inferno of Latin. Once Kanzo had spoken, his eyes turned violet; he was casting a spell that summoned a monstrous snake. It came rushing down the zipline toward the Techs. With viper speed, it snatched the drive.

"Noo!" Inferno and Volt both shouted.

Kanzo channelled his energy into a powerful blast, but just before it hit, Psych shielded them in a green sphere.

"My Lord is coming, and even you will be powerless against him," Kanzo shouted with a grin.

They made it back to the base, where everyone was waiting. Inferno and Volt were angry that they lost the drive. Psych, on the other hand, was awfully pleased with himself. He told them he had used the new update in the visors, and Volt and Ryku had installed and downloaded the file. Ryku rushed to the computer to download the file from his HUD, and there it was. With the data in front of them, they could now build the project Volt called REBIRTH.

"How are we going to build it?" Jet asked.

"Think of it as a DT project," Zach said.

Zach and Ryku went to the lab looking for all the spare circuit boards and metal they could find. Jet created a 3D version of what they were building with his powers. Ryku and Zach asked Kai to melt the metal into the shape of the canister, and Alex cooled it down. Ryku built the code for the release of the reversed particles. Zach powered it up. After two hours of construction, REBIRTH was finally complete.

The Ninja Techs had to bring it to the same spot as the Doomsday Device and release the new particles. Quake was the only one who was strong enough to carry REBIRTH, so he had the job of carrying it out of the base. Psych had to use his powers to create a lift for Quake to ascend to the top of Pearl Tower. Finally, in place, REBIRTH was ready to release the particles. Volt programmed it to 3 seconds, but the short time frame worried Psych.

"REBIRTH was designed to strip people of their powers. What does that mean for us?" he asked.

"REBIRTH was designed to eliminate corrupted energy. If my calculations are correct, we should be fine," Volt assured.

"But you're forgetting, we have had the most exposure to the corrupted energy. After all, we were in the middle of the blast," Subzero added.

"Well, if this is the end, it has meant the world to me to fight with you all," Quake said sadly.

They all huddled together, thinking this may be the last time they would ever be the Ninja Techs.

"Ok, REBIRTH is ready and the timer's set for 3 seconds. We did it," Volt concluded.

"And if this works, the government won't be able to make any super soldiers?" Inferno asked.

"No... they won't."

Three, two, one and the reversed particles were released. The particles lit up the sky in an array of colour and transformed all the people with corrupted energy back to their usual selves.

The Ninja Techs looked at one another, looking for signs that their powers were gone. Inferno took a breath and tested his power. It wasn't easy at first, but he started to feel the sensation—the heat coursing through him. He managed a spark. Then the spark turned into a mighty flame. They all cheered in celebration and shot bolts of their powers into the air.

VORAGON'S VENGEANCE

CHAPTER ELEVEN

Voragon's Vengeance

It had been a week since the element virus outbreak, and over 7 million people returned to their usual selves. The new school term had begun, and no Shifters or Kanzo were around to cause trouble. The team was in the middle of an algebra test with their teacher, Mrs. Davis. Kai and Jet sat in the class listening to Mrs. Davis drone on, waiting for something to get them out of it. That something came with a bang. The terrified look on the students' faces came with the inhaling of smoke and the bright red fury of the fire that exploded a quarter of the building. Kai rushed to the door, only to find it blocked by a heap of rubble on the other side.

"Hey!? Hello!? GET US OUT OF HERE!" He shouted while banging on the door.

Rocky quickly rushed to a window to open it.

"Quick! Out here!" Rocky shouted while coughing after inhaling some smoke.

All the students, including the teacher, didn't hesitate to leave. One by one, they leapt off, except the Ninja Techs. They had to find out what was going on and where the explosion came from. Rocky ran up to the door with his eyes glowing marigold like the light of the sun. With one quick movement, he demolished the door. Alex and Chloe combined their powers to put out the fires. With the fire out, the building was a steaming shell of rubble. A noise outside caught the attention of Kai and Alex. It sounded like a familiar voice to Kai.

"Jet, Rocky, Chloe, and Zach, help the injured get out while Alex and I go investigate," Kai commanded.

"Got it!" The rest said and went out to find the injured.

Kai and Alex made it outside. The sun was shining so bright that they initially had trouble making out what precisely the shadow form in front of them was. As their eyes adjusted, they saw a horned monster, his black cloak as dark as a lunar eclipse, with a purple energy running down it. The creature's lemon-yellow horns looked as sharp as a steel blade, and its eyes were violet and luminous, with smoke steaming out of its mouth like a fog machine.

They bravely walked toward the monster, transforming into their Ninja Tech gear as they approached.

"Hey, you exploded that building. Why?!" Inferno asked.

"To bring you here, Pax," The horned monster replied. The raspy voice and its implication sent a jolt of adrenaline through Inferno's core.

"You know who I am?"

"Who in the universe wouldn't know a member of the Pax family?"

"How do you know my family?"

"Your father and his team were legends to all, well respected and my most formidable rivals, but my father and I killed them."

Inferno couldn't believe what he heard. His anger was building.

"You're the one who killed my dad?" he asked, filled with rage; he charged up his energy, fury coursing through his veins and ready to explode. Inferno uncontrollably blasted him with all the fire he had, but the horned monster swatted the blast aside, and it shot into the sky.

"Who…Who are you?" Inferno asked, more afraid than he had ever been in his life.

"I go by many names. The Chaos Titan, The Young Overlord, Ruler of Planets, The Titan-Core Prince, but my most favoured is Voragon," he said with a grin that showed his razor-sharp fangs. His energy was like Kanzo's, but it was immensely powerful, as if it had the energy of the elements itself. He charged this god-like energy and roared loud enough to shake the heavens. He aimed at Inferno and shot a powerful blast of corrupted energy, but Quake made an earth wall to shield Inferno. Although the wall protected them, the explosion crumbled the wall into pieces. Inferno feared Voragon was almost invincible.

"Run while you still can. This is only the beginning. The next phase is coming—and everything you love will die by my hands," Voragon said, his voice eerily calm.

For once, the Ninjas had to retreat. The Ninja Techs quickly teleported away. They had never faced an opponent as strong as Voragon. They needed a plan. Kai figured that Ravena would know how to defeat him; he went straight to her to ask questions.

"Voragon is a major threat to the city," Rocky said exhaustedly. "He almost killed me and Kai back there."

"Look, my dad Voragon…" Raven started

"He's not your dad, Ravena." Kai interrupted, "Do you know what he did to our real one?"

"Yes… I do."

"So, you knew Voragon killed our dad, and you didn't even care enough to tell me?" Kai said, on the brink of exploding with anger.

"I'm sorry, Kai, I…"

"That's insane, Ravena!"

Kai blasted a powerful blast of fire at one of the punching bags. Ravena stepped back. Chloe went over to the ash-filled punching bag to put the fire out with her water.

"Kai, stand down. Ravena has been reunited with you after years under Voragon's control—and the only thing she remembers is that she's your sister.

It's not ok to snap at your sister like that." Alex tried to calm him down, but Kai was still angry, not just at Ravena but at Voragon as well.

"Look, I'm sorry about your father, but don't forget all our parents were on that team too, and they died with him. So, right now we need to stop him so he can't do this to anyone else, and they won't have to feel the way you do. Ok?" Alex asked.

"Ok, Ravena. I'm sorry," Kai apologised and hugged her.

"How do we stop him?" Alex asked calmly.

"Let me tell you everything I know," Ravena began.

CHAPTER TWELVE

How It Began, How It Will End

"I will tell you about Voragon and how it all began," Ravena began to tell them all she knew.

"Long ago, when time first began, the elements were born on a planet called Elementia, and it was said to be beautiful. All the people who lived there with the dragons were related to an element, but there was one that was more powerful than the others— the legendary Universal Element. The Universal Element only belonged to one family. That was the Pax family, my family. The firstborn son or daughter inherits the power in each generation, which means Kai has this element within him. Voragon came from a planet whose name was lost in time. The dragons feared the place more than any, and left them, too afraid to even say its name, so Elementia gave it the name Titan's Core. The planet was inhabited by core-draining beasts—creatures that absorbed the energy of other planets' cores to gain elemental power. The most powerful of all was Elementia's core, the very heart of the elements. That's why Kilojav, the leader of Titan's Core and Voragon's father, set his sights on it. Then came the invasion.

"The first Universal Master, Grand-Master Korven, had to form an army of the most powerful elements: ice, water, earth, electricity, energy, and fire. Sadly, the entire race of those elements died in that war. Grand-Master Korven needed an advantage, so he used some of his elemental energy to create a master of five of the six elements, leaving fire for himself. Grand-Master Korven honoured the element and used it for himself. Doing this made the first team that would last generations, the Elementals. They were a force to be reckoned with, nearly impossible to stop. They managed to fight the Core-Eaters and drive them away, but the planet was shaking, and buildings were driven to the ground. Grand-Master Korven thought the Core-Eaters absorbed the core. Without thinking, he and the master of energy created a ship for the rest of the races to survive on a new planet, Earth.

"The Elementals made a life for themselves on their new home planet, coexisting in peace with the dinosaurs, and soon after, humans. Grand-Master Korven declared that he and the Elementals would protect this planet for generations to come and would not lose this planet like they lost Elementia. Since then, the mantle has been passed on for millennia."

"Ok, nice story, but how does that help us with our Voragon problem?" Jet asked.

"Voragon has absorbed enough cores to make his corrupted energy, element-infused, and himself nearly invulnerable," Ravena said. "But all cores are filled with heat energy, making him warm-blooded. So, frigid temperatures can freeze the heat in him and destroy him. That is why, Alex, you will be the one to defeat him."

"I can't. Even I don't have that amount of ice," Alex admitted.

"Use Ice Burst Jutsu," Kai suggested.

The Ninja Techs were speechless at the thought of using Jutsu. None of them managed to use it.

"Ok, if that's what it takes, I have to try!" Alex said.

"Guys, Alex isn't the only one who needs training! So does Nikki and Zoey!" Chloe said.

"Right, let's bring on the training!" Kai decided.

13

NEW KIDS ON THE BLOCK

CHAPTER THIRTEEN

New Kids on The Block

Chloe, Zoey, and Nikki were walking down the street because Chloe had something to tell them.

"Do you still have your powers?" she asked.

"Yes, why?" they both asked in unison.

"My friends and I have wanted to tell you something for a while now," she said excitedly, "Hope you're ready!"

Nikki and Zoey were confused, but they didn't have time to think, as Chloe teleported them to the Ninja Tech Base, where Kai, Rocky, Jet, Zach, and Alex were fully suited.

"Hey Kai. Hey Jet!" Nikki said excitedly.

The Ninja Techs frowned at Kai while Zoey stood confused.

"You told her?" Volt groaned.

"In my defence, she found out on her own," Inferno replied.

"We're in the Ninja Tech Base!" Zoey asked, "Wait, why are we here?"

"We brought you here so we can train you with your new powers." Chloe said, "Let's get started."

Inferno and Psych rushed over to the computer to prepare the training circle. When they said the voice code "Grid Awaken", the circular floor instantly glowed and lifted into a circle.

"Let's rock!" Psych shouted excitedly.

"But before we do, we need to get you some suits," Inferno said.

"Luckily, the Resistance had some ready for you." Ryku handed them the Tech Watches.

"What are you going to call yourself?" Psych asked.

Nikki grabbed her Tech Watch, put it on and transformed. She had a scarlet-red hood and a purple, mouth-covering mask with an embroidered cape.

"Scarlet Hex, but you can call me Hex for short."

Zoey put hers on next. When she transformed, her suit was white and green.

"How about Ghost? Because I can go through walls and teleport," Zoey said.

Now they were ready to train. Inferno and Psych brought them up to the training circle. As Hex was walking up to the platform, Ravena stopped her.

"Before you go, take this," she said.

"A book?" Scarlet Hex asked.

"Not just any book, this is a mage spell book."

"What does it do?"

"There are four types of magic: Basic, Light, Dark, which is me, and Shadowmancy, which is you. Say your magic, and it will go onto the pages of your magic runes and Latin words."

"Shadowmancy?" Hex said nervously.

The spell book then glowed purple and floated out of her hands. It flicked through the pages rapidly until it found the chapter on Shadowmancy. It was covered in various spell runes, each inscribed with its Latin incantations.

"Wow, thanks," Scarlet Hex said.

"Now, take my brother down," Ravena smiled.

It was Inferno and Psych versus Hex and Ghost. Inferno lit a fire starter, and the circle became the Circle of Ash. The fire swerved around the pit, making it impossible to get out.

"To win, you must defeat us, which is very difficult," Psych bragged, "I wish you good luck."

Ghost teleported into Psych, kicking him in the face.

"Strange, that wasn't very difficult," Ghost smirked.

Hex got out her spell book and said the words "Inanis" while tracing the rune. Inferno almost got pulled into the eclipse of a portal but instinctively flipped out. Ghost, however, was too fast for Psych. He had to speed up.

"You've got a need for speed? Well, so do I!" he shouted, rocketing toward her with lightning speed. His energy-forged jet boots blazed as he charged, hurling jolts of electricity in every direction. Inferno, however, was doing his best to stay on his feet. Hex was quickly learning the skills of her power and the spell book.

"Good. You're doing well," Inferno said.

"Learning from the best," Hex replied.

"I think that's enough training for today," Psych said, trying to catch his breath.

"Yeah. Ok, sure," Ghost said.

At that moment, the alarm went off. Something was going on at a construction site. The Ninja Techs had some trouble to deal with. Inferno and the team were ready, but he noticed on Hex and Ghost's faces that they wanted to come.

"Hey guys, time for the real deal," Inferno said.

They smiled and got themselves ready. The Ninja Techs arrived at the site to find that Kanzo had come prepared. He had upgraded Shifters into what he called Sentinels.

"Ninja, say hello to my friends. This time, you will meet your match." Kanzo grinned.

"Wait, you have friends?" Psych asked, raising an eyebrow.

"Oh, that's colder than me," Subzero laughed.

Kanzo's eyes narrowed.

"You won't be laughing after this." Kanzo shouted, "Sentinels!"

"Sub, Scarlett and Ghost, go for Kanzo, the others and I can handle the Sentinels," Inferno said.

They nodded and ran at Kanzo. Subzero came in, freezing Kanzo's hands and legs, binding them together. Ghost teleported into Kanzo, beating him up left and right. Then Hex was ready for her turn. She used a spell to create tendril arms, by saying the incantation "multi bracchium". Midnight black tendrils awoke from the sandy ground, entangling Kanzo in it. Inferno and the rest were having fun toying with the Sentinels.

"Psych, trip rope," Inferno chuckled.

Psych smirked as he made a tripwire between the two of them. Then Wave lured two of the Sentinels down the path where the trip rope was. They tripped and flipped onto the floor, which was when Wave made a water slide for them to slide down. Volt and Quake were zapping and smashing the other three, having a great time doing it. Volt charged up many electrical balls of energy and shot them at the Sentinels, while Quake used his stone-covered hands to slap them back and forth. Subzero, Hex, and Ghost were standing their ground, but Kanzo was strong. They would have to combine their powers into one.

"You ready, team?" Subzero asked.

"Ready," Hex and Ghost responded.

Ghost grabbed Hex and Subzero's wrists and teleported them right in front of Kanzo. The three of them delivered a tri-powered punch at him. The impact ripped some of Kanzo's robe. As quickly as he came, he ran away. The Sentinels also vanished in a puff of smoke, giving the Ninja Techs a chance to regroup.

"Kanzo was down, but he escaped. I planted a tracker on him," Subzero said.

"We need to find out what Voragon is planning. Take Hex and Ghost with you," Inferno replied.

Subzero nodded, and the three of them followed the tracker.

"While they're out, we should head for the Resistance Base and tell them about what we know," Volt said.

14

WRATH OF THE SENTINELS

CHAPTER FOURTEEN

Wrath of the Sentinels

Subzero, Hex and Ghost were following Kanzo quietly like shadows. He was going to what looked like a small factory. Kanzo went through a door around the back, and Hex was about to follow him until Subzero froze the door. She looked at him, confused, but then he pointed up at an open window on the roof. She nodded, and they climbed up to the top. They quietly jumped down onto the roof. The factory had emerald-green windows, and somewhere inside, they could hear the whir of a large power generator. Hex spied a squad of Shifters patrolling. They would have to be quiet. Beyond the Shifters was an army of Sentinels lined up like mindless drones. They were not active, but Kanzo was mass-producing them. It looked like Voragon was preparing for his endgame. Subzero knew he had to destroy the factory.

"We need to get to the generator. If I get close enough, I could hack into the systems and shut the whole thing down," he explained.

"I'll teleport in and open the door," Ghost said.

"Not that simple," he said while scanning for obstacles on his Tech Bracer. "Those sensors will detect your elemental energy, so we will have to do this the old-fashioned way, by getting the keycard. Hex, can you clone yourself with an illusion spell, then Ghost can teleport and grab the card from that main Shifter?"

"Duplicare," Hex whispered as she traced the rune from her spell book. Clones of Hex appeared.

"Distract them," she whispered.

The clones swirled in front of the guards, hovering like drones, luring them around a wall, where Subzero lay in wait to freeze them into a solid block of ice.

"Keycard?" Subzero asked.

Ghost held the keycard with two fingers. "Keycard," she grinned.

The team unlocked the door with the keycard. Subzero saw the code for the device that powers the Sentinels and started hacking. Unfortunately, the Shifters escaped his ice encasing, so Hex and Ghost had to fight them off. Moving like lightning, they dodged incoming punches while making instinctive counters. Hex embraced her inner Shadowmancy abilities, knocking Shifters back.

"Nice job!" Ghost said.

"Thanks, you too," Hex replied.

"We should check on Sub."

"Yeah, let's go."

Subzero tried every combination but was unable to turn it off. They were going to have to do the very thing Subzero did not want to do: which was to destroy it. Hex checked the book of runes for a spell to destroy it without casualties. She heard something calling to her.

"Use the Void Strike spell," it whispered.

The book glowed and flicked to the page.

"Huh…Wha…"

Confused and heavy with hesitation, Hex had no other idea. She raised her arms, conjuring the spell while pulling all shadow energy towards her.

"Inanis Percutiens," She muttered.

"Hex, what are you doing?" Subzero's brows furrowed.

Her powers were like an infection inside her waiting to burst. Channelling all that power, Hex unleashed a surge of energy, breaking the primary device, which then exploded, killing the Shifters and the Sentinels. Suddenly, the walls began to crack, and the roof started to crumble.

"The building's collapsing. Let's go," Subzero shouted.

Subzero, Hex, and Ghost all made it out the same way they came, leaving nothing but a smoking factory behind. In a flash, Ghost, Hex and Subzero teleported back into the base.

"There you are," Zach smiled.

"What happened to you?" Rocky asked with a puzzled face.

"Long story. I'll tell you later," Subzero replied while trying to catch his breath.

"Anyways, there are some strange readings on Voragon's ship. He is preparing for his endgame, so we must be one step ahead of him," Kai explained. "Kanzo's ship is still here. If we send a team to investigate, we could determine what Voragon is planning and prepare to counter it. But we will need the Resistance's help."

"Jet and I will meet up with the Resistance," Chloe said.

"Let's end this!" Rocky grinned.

15

OPERATION: INFILTRATION

CHAPTER FIFTEEN

Operation: Infiltration

High on the roof of a tall building, Inferno, Quake, Volt, and Subzero stalked the airship, waiting for the perfect moment to swoop in. After a few seconds of waiting, Inferno gave the signal. In a flash, the Ninja Techs used a zipline up to the ship. They knew they were close when they saw Kanzo marching down the hallway with two Sentinels and four Shifters behind him.

"Can you scan for the planning room?" Inferno whispered.

Volt activated his visor and looked around. "Found it. Sending the location to your visors now, put them on."

They put their visors on and crept up to the upper floor into the planning room. "We made it. Look around for their plans," Inferno said.

"It could be on paper or drives or something alien. I can't tell," Volt said, searching thoroughly.

While Inferno, Quake, and Subzero looked through their over-equipped boxes, Volt skimmed through Kanzo's systems.

"Hey! I've finally found something. Check this out," Volt said.

The Ninja Techs came over and looked at the screen.

"You see this design, it's like the Doomsday Device, only it's much worse. It seems to use Voragon's power to amplify an energy drill to reach not only Earth's core, but also to drain the elemental energy infused within it," Volt explained.

"It's like what Raven said. He's going to absorb the core's energy," Inferno said.

"We won't let that happen," Quake said.

Then one noise made them freeze: Alarms were ringing. Kanzo had found them. Inferno could hear the massive number of Shifters coming their way. Adrenaline pulsed through him, triggering his powers. His eyes shifted into a clear white colour. Kanzo then opened the doors to find Inferno floating in the air, charging up some new kind of energy.

"Guys, get behind me," Inferno commanded, his voice eerily calm under the circumstances.

The wind was swirling around him, and this power produced a cyclone of wind that blasted Kanzo and his soldiers, knocking them out for a few moments. Volt checked their camera network and saw that more of the Sentinels and Shifters were heading their way. They had to get back to base. As they ran, Inferno saw the main power room. He stopped, falling behind the rest of the group. If he could blow it up, it would stop their plans and communication.

"Get to the zipline," Volt shouted.

Volt balanced his Nanotech Zip Baton in the middle of the zipline and slid down along with Quake and Subzero, who were right behind him, but Inferno was still on the ship.

"Dude, now is not the time!" Volt shouted.

"I could blow it up!" Inferno shouted back. "I could stop this!"

"What?!"

"I must try! I'll see you at base."

Inferno went back in. Subzero let go of his baton, falling from the zipline. He made an ice path back to the ship.

"What are you doing?!" Quake shouted.

"Saving his butt," Subzero said.

Inferno was ready, as was Kanzo with eight Sentinels behind him.

"Come on, powers. Hit me with something new," Inferno muttered.

A rush of electricity flowed, charging up through him and his eyes. He leapt towards Kanzo and let out a surge of electric power, knocking out two Sentinels. He knew this power was uncontrollable as he looked around, seeing that the walls and roof were covered with the ashy spots that the electricity had hit. Kanzo was angry and lashed his power at him, but Inferno was trained well and found ways to dodge his attacks. Uncontrollably, a gust of wind flowed from his fist at Kanzo, knocking him unconscious. He leapt over Kanzo and ran through the airship to find the primary power source. After searching for a few minutes, Inferno found the room. He looked around for a way to shut it down, but there were no power buttons. Then the realisation kicked in harder than a football to the head: he had to do it manually. He closed his eyes and focused solely on the strongest fire he had ever produced. The energy swirled around him as before, like a cyclone that was on fire. Before he could strike, Kanzo and his Sentinels came barging in.

"What are you DOING?!" Kanzo roared angrily.

"Saving Earth." Inferno laughed and, within a flash, he struck the core with all his power. Kanzo teleported away, leaving the Sentinels to perish in the flames. The explosion obliterated the ship, sending rubble hurtling down into the city. Through the smoke and falling debris, Inferno plummeted unconscious from the sky. He would not wake up. His chances of survival were low, and it looked like the end for him.

THE PURENESS OF WHITE

CHAPTER SIXTEEN

The Pureness of White

Things were looking grim for Inferno—his suit was torn, ash streaked his skin, and he was scorched from head to toe. But then, a familiar cold sensation crept in.

"I've got you, Kai," a familiar voice said.

It was Subzero! He came in on his icy slide and carried him carefully and cautiously back to base.

"You're back, little bro," Zach smiled.

"Yeah, we thought you were dead," Jet said.

"One of us might be," Subzero said, transforming back, then showing them their injured friend. The room stilled. The chatter that had filled the base had turned to a sombre hollow void.

"I'm going to kill them all," Jet fumed.

"No, stick to the plan Kai made. You must go see the Resistance," Rocky said.

"Put him in the Medical Room in my lab," Zach gestured to the exam table.

Rocky and Alex carried Kai into the Medical Room while Chloe and Jet contacted Ronin to warn them of their incoming arrival. They had their Tech Watches ready and locked onto the Resistance base, so they transformed and teleported.

When they got to the base, they wasted no time telling them about Kai and Voragon's plans. While they were shocked about what happened to Kai, Ronin didn't look surprised as they discussed Voragon's plans. Ronin led them to the training room, where Jet and Chloe saw two new Resistance members training. Jet took in the new Ninja's powers. He saw a dark and light blue Ninja Tech training with magical abilities, a steel grey that could manipulate metal. Jet was almost caught off guard when he found himself staring at Ninja Tech's first enemy.

"Wait, Crystal?" Jet's reaction was to blast the known enemy with energy bullets. She easily dodged them.

"Hold it, Jet. She's on our side now," Ronin said.

"How?"

"She was captured and corrupted by Kanzo and sent as a mind-controlled enemy," Ronin explained. "Anyway, I'd like you to meet our new members, Steel, the Elemental of Metal Manipulation, except platinum, Presto, Elemental of Basic Magic. The Resistance has your backs, Ninja Techs."

The Resistance then saluted Jet and Chloe with smiles on their faces. Jet and Chloe saluted back at them.

Meanwhile, back at base, Zach was working on defence and offence modifications on their weapons. Alex came into the lab looking very worried.

"Hey, got a minute?" Alex asked.

"Yeah sure. What's up?" Zach replied.

"We're all preparing for the battle, and I know I'm the one who has to defeat Voragon, but if something happens… If I don't make it, I… I love you, bro and promise me that you'll be ok if I'm gone."

Zach sighed. He put his screwdriver away, sat Alex down, and put his hand on his shoulder.

"Alex, look at me, nothing and I mean nothing will take you away. I promised Mom and Dad that I would protect you, and I am not breaking that promise at all." He smiled and hugged him tightly.

After their talk, they went to see if Kai had woken up yet. He was still unconscious. Alex knew that Voragon was nearly here and that they had to do it without Kai. It would take the whole team. So, he called everyone with his Tech Watch and told the other Ninja Techs and the Resistance to suit up and meet up on the roof. Looking out at the city from the rooftops, the team could tell the battle had already come. The sky was on fire and filled with smoke and ashes. Cars were burning, and people were stuck in buildings. Citizens were either screaming to be saved or running from danger. Hundreds of Sentinels came marching through the streets. "This is looking bad, guys," Quake said as he looked out over the city.

"We've had some close calls, but this is something else," Psych sighed.

Subzero turned around to face the team. "I can't believe what I'm hearing," Subzero said. "We're the Ninja Techs."

"Being the Ninja Techs isn't enough anymore. We lost Kai, and we're risking our lives when we're thirteen!" Quake argued.

Everyone stood in silence.

"Voragon is the biggest threat we've faced, and I know we are afraid, but our parents died to protect people. The fate of the world is in the hands of the only people who can help us. We may be thirteen, we may have lost Kai, but you know what, we still have hope." Subzero straightened up as he looked each of them in the eye.

"You know what, you're right," Psych said.

"We're a team now," Wave smiled.

"Ok, listen up. The Resistance will rescue the people and escort them to Brooklyn. Volt and Jet will stop the device. Quake, and hopefully Inferno if he wakes, will handle the Sentinel and Shifter army. Wave and I must defeat Voragon. Let's do this, Ninja Techs."

The Ninja Techs nodded and jumped off the roof. At that moment, a Sentinel looked up, only to be knocked out by Quake. Quake hit stone blasts at each of the Shifters, and when they were staggered, he encased them in stone spheres. Subzero and Wave were perched on lamp posts looking for Voragon.

Volt and Psych were hidden in an alleyway. Their hearts were pounding at the thought that they would mess this up, as they could see Kanzo and some Sentinels underneath the train tracks preparing the device. They quietly snuck behind two Sentinels and made a swift takedown. Then Volt and Psych jumped up to the roof of the elevated train tracks. Kanzo looked behind him, thinking he would catch a Ninja Tech and destroy one. Just the thought was enough to make him laugh.

***

Quake pulled his arm back to punch another Shifter in the face. He was a beast, smashing all of them with his stone hands, but the thing that made him smirk was that they kept coming for more.

***

Subzero and Wave found Voragon waiting in the middle of the double-tracked railway, standing motionless like he was waiting for something or someone. Subzero was about to jump in, but Wave stopped him.

"We should go in quietly," she whispered.

Subzero nodded, and they crept towards Voragon to avoid detection, but then they were caught off guard when he yelled, "PAX, COME OUT AND FACE ME!"

"He wants to fight with Kai, but why?" Wave whispered.

"Kai's dad is the Universal Master and Voragon's biggest rival. Because Kai is the oldest child, he is now the Universal Master's successor, so I guess Voragon wants to get rid of the element—or he has a huge grudge." Subzero whispered back.

Subzero and Wave jumped down onto the tracks to try and fight Voragon without causing mass destruction to the surroundings.

***

At the same time, Volt and Psych incapacitated the rest of the Sentinels, leaving Kanzo unprotected still preparing the drill.

"Hey Kanzo," Psych taunted.

Kanzo immediately turned around to face them.

"Do you know what Volt plus Psych equals?" Volt asked smugly.

Kanzo narrowed his eyes but shook his head slowly. Volt and Psych then blasted him with their combined elements, which made Kanzo look like an ashy, singed monster.

"Your worst nightmare," Psych laughed. Volt tried to shut down the drill while Psych made a sphere around them so that no Shifters or Sentinels could get in.

***

Quake was in trouble, he was overwhelmed by a dozen Shifters, each one relentlessly trying to beat him down. But just in time, Presto from the Resistance summoned a whirlwind, blasting the attackers away in a surge of wind and power. Quake shook Presto's hand and said, "Thanks for the help, uh…"

"You can call me Presto."

***

Back on the tracks, Subzero and Wave were about to attack, but Voragon turned around, his eyes glowing purple, and a wispy mist crept out of them. He used a corrupted blast to injure Wave and Subzero, knocking them down. Neither of them could move, let alone defend themselves.

Voragon menacingly walked up to Wave, narrowing his eyes and yelling, "YOU SEND ME THIS TO TRY AND KILL ME, PAX! Watch as I make an example out of them!"

He raised his glowing hand toward Wave, corrupted energy building in the palm of his hand. Suddenly, a Ninja flipped down. His hands glowed as bright as the sun as they sliced Voragon's hand off. Voragon, screaming in agony, realised along with Subzero and Wave that this person wasn't just a Ninja, it was Inferno!

"Missed me?" he asked smugly.

Voragon roared with rage. Subzero and Wave's injuries healed fast. They got back up on their feet and joined Inferno.

"Wave, help Quake. Subzero and I can handle this." Inferno didn't take his eyes off Voragon.

As Voragon slowly got up, his hand regenerated. Inferno shot as many fire blasts as he could, turning all his anger into focus. Subzero then froze Voragon's legs together and shot an ice blast directly at his face. Inferno and Subzero decided to blast him together, combining fire and ice as one. One by one, they shot explosions of fire and ice, which brought Voragon down to his knees.

***

Volt was trying to shut down the device, but Kanzo and a dozen Sentinels were blasting the sphere to weaken it.

"Hurry up, Volt," Psych said, straining to keep the sphere up.

"What do you think I'm doing?" Volt argued, trying to think. He had an idea. He put both hands on the keyboard and charged his electricity. He paired his Tech Bracer with the device to scan for a shutdown code. The moment he found it, the shield was down, and Kanzo and his army charged through. Psych did what he could to stop them, but it wasn't enough. Quake and Wave both saw Psych unsuccessfully fend off the Sentinels. They ran over to stop them but found themselves overrun with Shifters.

***

Voragon charged up his dark energy and slammed his palms onto the ground, causing a powerful shockwave that knocked Inferno away. Subzero quickly caught him by shooting a line from his grappling glove that wrapped around his foot. The shockwave was so powerful that the wind was swirling around like a tornado, trying to send Inferno flying. He looked down and saw Psych, Quake, and Wave fending off an entire army. They still needed help.

"Subzero, I need to go and help them," he said.

"I can't beat Voragon without you," Subzero replied.

"Yes, you can. You're a Ninja Tech, and we never give up."

"But...how do I beat him?"

"It's like my sister said, Ice Burst Jutsu."

Inferno transported his Laser Sword, cut the line on his foot, and dived down, landing with a massive punch to the ground. His flaming fist sent licks of fire out, burning up four dozen Shifters.

Now Inferno, Wave, Psych, and Quake had to hold back the army from reaching Volt and the drill. Volt had the shutdown code, but a better idea came to mind. He charged some electricity into the computer with one hand, then typed a new code with the other. His plan was almost ready to go, but he needed one last thing.

"Psych, shield up!" Volt shouted. Psych nodded and made a rectangular barrier in front of them. Volt front-flipped over the shield and used his electricity to absorb five of the Shifter's energy. Volt was screaming in agony; his powers were storing a quarter of the Shifters' corrupted energy, and it was a painful experience. Once he had enough of their energy, he went back to the device and charged it up with the Shifters' energy. Psych once again could not keep the shield up any longer, but he didn't need to. Volt's new code was built. He activated the device. Quake panicked and shouted, "Volt, wait, don't!", but it was too late.

At that moment, the device emitted a bright, light-blue beam that blasted into the air. All the Sentinels and Shifters exploded into purple particles that were sucked into the beam. Volt made a code that would scan for Shifter energy and pull it back into the device in its original form.

"What's happening? What did you Do?!" Kanzo cried.

"Exploded all your Shifters. Now you're on your own." Volt laughed.

Inferno, the distracted Kanzo was hit by a massive wave of fire that singed his clothes. Kanzo was eager to destroy the Ninja Techs, but he knew he was defeated. He teleported away.

***

Subzero was still battling Voragon on the railway. Subzero threw ice balls at Voragon's head, which pushed him back. He ran at him and kicked him in the face, then used the momentum from running to move away from his attacks. Subzero transported his Tech Bow and Quiver and shot two arrows at Voragon's feet. Voragon roared with laughter at the fact he missed, but then the arrows released smoke that swirled around him, obscuring his vision. Voragon roared, and the sound blew the smoke away just in time for Voragon to get a glance of Subzero charging at him with a powerful ice punch to his face. Voragon staggered backwards, and Subzero knew it was time to end this. Subzero felt the balance between calm and fear, and felt those emotions fuel him instead of holding him back.

"You are no master, yet you are lethal in combat. Who are you?" Voragon asked angrily, trying to get back up.

"I'm Subzero, the White Ninja Tech, and I'm about to do this," he said, running directly towards him, not stopping, determined to defeat him.

He focused on summoning and connecting with the energy swirling inside him, and with complete confidence, he yelled, "Ice Burst Jutsu!"

In a flash, a spire you could see from miles, made solely of ice, formed around them. Inside was a raging blizzard colder than Antarctica, and only Subzero and Voragon were encased. Subzero's eyes glowed a light blue colour as the blizzard swirled around him. His fingers were covered in nothing but ice, like his normal hands did not exist. Voragon, still trying to recover from Subzero's ice punch, blasted a direct strike at him, but Subzero's emotions were so balanced that the blast was frozen solid. Subzero flew towards Voragon, determined to end this. He shoved his icy fingers deeply inside his chest. Voragon was paralysed because of Subzero's grip. In that moment, the blizzard started to pass through Subzero's body like it was energising him.

"This is our world, and we protect it," Subzero told him.

Voragon was still struggling to move. He could feel the frost of the cold embrace of upcoming death. Voragon could not escape.

"You think this is the end; there will be others. My father will kill you. You will remember what I have said." Voragon gasped for air.

Subzero chuckled lightly. "Then the Ninja Techs won't stop until we've defeated them all."

Subzero blasted all the ice energy he had through Voragon, who was roaring in agony; he was frozen from the inside out, becoming an ice statue. In the last moments, Subzero punched the statue. It shattered into a million pieces, and it was done. Subzero had defeated Voragon. The ice spire that the Ice Burst Jutsu had raised began to melt away. Subzero gently floated down to the ground where the team was waiting for him. They all cheered for Subzero. They had just won against Voragon and saved Earth. They took their masks off to get some fresh air from the night sky.

"You did it, Alex," Kai said proudly.

"You are amazing, brother." Volt smiled before hugging him tightly.

In that moment, a glowing trench coat in the colours of ice materialised on Alex.

"This is what the Tech Scroll meant by the trench coat. You are now the Elemental Master of Ice!" Volt slapped Alex on the back.

***

Not too far away, Kanzo was limping towards them, filled with rage. He had a blast, charged up in his hand, ready to shoot one of them.

"You will pay for killing the Titan-Core Prince," Kanzo muttered to himself.

He aimed closely at Alex and slowly shot the blast. In that exact second, Kai looked at Kanzo, and Alex was struck.

"Noo!" Inferno yelled before blasting Kanzo with an immense amount of fire, which brought him to the ground. Kanzo's shot had hit Subzero's back. He was screaming as blood leaked from his back, staining the white of his Ninja suit. Inferno's mind was racing, his brain trying to find a way to save him. Volt knelt next to him, more scared than anyone else.

"You're going to be ok, you hear me. Everything is going to be ok," Volt cried.

Subzero smiled and used the little strength he had to hold Volt's hand and said in a weak voice, "I love you…brother."

Volt, feeling so guilty, replied, "I love you, too, Alex."

Subzero stopped breathing. Volt felt a barrage of emotions: guilt, anger, sadness and fear.

"I can fix this, I can do something, I have to be able to do something, I…" he cried.

Wave knelt beside him and placed her hand on his shoulder. Psych, Quake, and Inferno stood in silence. With Subzero becoming weaker and weaker and the hope of saving him slipping away, it looked like the sad end of Alexander Bolteson, the Elemental Master of Ice.

To Be Continued…

The Ninja Techs Return In:

ISSUE 2
Elemental Ninja Techs:
Sailors of the Sky